DRAGON

Gets By

Read the complete DRAGON series!

DRAGON

Gets By

DAV PILKEY

ACORN™
SCHOLASTIC

For my old pal George Hurst

Published in the UK by Scholastic Children's Books, 2020
Euston House, 24 Eversholt Street, London, NW1 1DB, UK

A division of Scholastic Limited.
London – New York – Toronto – Sydney – Auckland
Mexico City – New Delhi – Hong Kong
SCHOLASTIC and associated logos are trademarks and/or
registered trademarks of Scholastic Inc.
First published in the US by Orchard Books, 1991
This edition first published in the US by Scholastic Inc, 2020
Text and illustration© Dav Pilkey, 1991, 2020

The right of Dav Pilkey to be identified as the author and illustrator of this work has
been asserted by him under the Copyright, Designs and Patents Act 1988.

ISBN 978 0 702 30165 0

A CIP catalogue record for this book is available from the British Library.

Printed by CPI Group (UK) Ltd, Croydon, CR0 4YY
Papers used by Scholastic Children's Books are made
from wood grown in sustainable forests.
1 3 5 7 9 10 8 6 4 2

This is a work of fiction. Names, characters, places, incidents
and dialogues are products of the author's imagination or are used
fictitiously. Any resemblance to actual people, living or dead,
events or locales is entirely coincidental.

www.scholastic.co.uk

Contents

1
Dragon Sees the Day

One warm, sunny morning
Dragon woke up and yawned.
He was very groggy...
And whenever Dragon woke up groggy,
he did **everything** wrong.

First, he read an egg
and fried the morning newspaper.

Then he buttered his tea
and sipped a cup of toast.

Finally, Dragon opened the door
to see the day.
But Dragon did not see the sun.
He did not see the trees or the hills
or the flowers or the sky.
He saw only shadows.

"It must still be night-time,"
said Dragon.

So he went back to bed.

2
Housework

Dragon's floor was very dirty.
He got his broom and began to sweep.

When he was finished sweeping,
the floor was still dirty.

So Dragon swept again...
And there was still dirt everywhere.

"There sure is a lot of dirt
on this floor," said Dragon.

Dragon swept all morning long,
and into the afternoon.
He carried out wheelbarrows
filled with dirt.

All of his sweeping left
a very big hole in his floor.

Finally, the postmouse came by.
She looked at all the dirt
outside the house.

She looked at the big hole
inside the house.

"What's going on in here?"
asked the postmouse.

"I'm sweeping my floor," said Dragon.
"It is very dirty."

"But you have a dirt floor,"
said the postmouse.
"It is made of dirt."

Dragon looked at the hole he had swept,
and scratched his big head.

"Looks like you've made a mess,"
said the postmouse.

"Looks like I've made a basement,"
said Dragon.

3
Yardwork

Dragon looked at the big pile of dirt
in his yard.
"What am I going to do with all this dirt?"
he wondered.

He got a shovel
and dug a big, deep hole.

Then he scooped the dirt into the hole.

"Well, that takes care of that,"
said Dragon.

4
Shopping

Dragon looked in his cupboard,
but there was no food at all.

"The cupboard is bare," said Dragon.
"Time to go shopping."

Dragon got into his car and drove.
The food store was at the top of a hill.
It was a very steep drive.

Dragon loved to go shopping.
He was a very wise shopper.
He bought food only from
the five basic food groups:

He bought cheese curls
from the dairy group.
He bought doughnuts
from the bread group.

And he bought fudge pops
from the chocolate group.

Dragon had a balanced diet.

He had so much food that he could not
fit it all into his car.

"I know what I will do," said Dragon.
"I will eat some of the food now,
and then the rest will fit in the car."

Dragon sat in the car park
and started to eat.
He crunched up the cheese curls.
He downed the doughnuts.
He packed away the pork scratchings.
Dragon ate and ate and ate
until all the food was gone.

"Burp!"

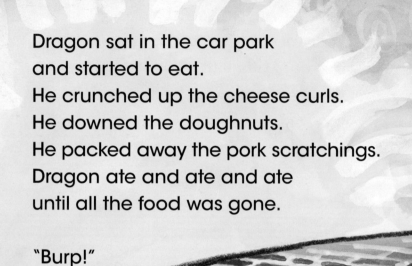

Now **Dragon** could not fit into his car.

"Oh, what am I going to do?"
cried Dragon.

He thought and thought,
and scratched his big head.

41

"I know what I will do," said Dragon.
"I will push my car home."

So Dragon pushed his car down the hill.

The car began to roll faster and faster...

. . . and faster . . .

. . . and faster.

Finally, Dragon's car came to a stop right in front of his house.

All the excitement had made Dragon
very hungry.
He went into his kitchen
and looked in the cupboard.
There was no food at all.

"The cupboard is bare," said Dragon.
"Time to go shopping."

5
Good Night, Dragon

It had been a long, busy day,
and now it was bedtime.

Dragon was very groggy.
So he brushed his head
and combed his teeth . . .

He watered his bed...

. . . crawled into his plants . . .

. . . and fell fast asleep.

About the Author

Dav Pilkey is the creator of the bestselling Dog Man and Captain Underpants series. He has written and illustrated many other books for young readers, including the Dumb Bunnies series, *The Hallo-Wiener*, *Dog Breath*, and *The Paperboy*, which is a Caldecott Honour book. Dav lives in the Pacific Northwest with his wife.

YOU CAN DRAW DRAGON!

① Draw a letter "C" and a small arch. They should connect.

② Add Dragon's eyes, nose, and smile. Put two horns on top of his head.

③ Draw Dragon's back and tail.

④ Add Dragon's tummy and one of his feet.

5 Draw Dragon's arms and hands. Don't forget to add his other foot!

6 Draw spikes down his back and on his tail.

7 Add a flower and some grass. Dragon is sniffing the flower!

8 Colour in your drawing!

WHAT'S YOUR STORY?

Dragon makes a lot of mistakes when he is groggy.
Imagine **you** did not get enough sleep last night.
What mistakes would you make?
Where would you take a nap?
Write and draw your story!

BONUS!

Try making your story just like Dav –
with watercolours! Did you know that
Dav taught himself how to watercolour
when he was making the Dragon books?
He went to the supermarket, bought a children's watercolour
set, and used it to paint the entire book series.